The Dog Who Insisted He Wasn't

by Marilyn Singer / illustrated by Kelly Oechsli

A TRUMPET CLUB SPECIAL EDITION

Published by The Trumpet Club
666 Fifth Avenue, New York, New York 10103

Text copyright © 1976 by Marilyn Singer
Illustrations copyright © 1976 by Kelly Oechsli

ISBN: 0-440-84257-3

This edition published by arrangement with Marilyn Singer
Designed by Meri Shardin
Printed in the United States of America
November 1990

10 9 8 7 6 5 4 3 2 1
DP

To my own Konrad,
  and his good friend, Saskia

Konrad was a dog—but he refused to believe it.

His mother had told him, "Konrad, you're such a handsome dog."

"Hmm-hmm-hmm-hmm-hmm," sang Konrad so he didn't have to listen.

One day he was adopted by a family who wanted a dog. They treated Konrad just the way a dog should be treated. He had two bright plastic dishes—one for dog food and one for water. He had a comfortable piece of rug, a shiny collar, a long leather leash. He was walked and brushed, patted on the head, and given chewy biscuits. For any dog, it was a wonderful life. But not for Konrad. As far as he was concerned, it was a dog's life and he wasn't a dog!

So, he ran away.

The street was full of people, all of whom he approached with what he thought was a smile. "What a nice dog," everyone said.

"But I'm not a dog," answered Konrad.

"He must be lost."

"I'm not lost. I ran away."

"Such a friendly dog too—maybe I'll take him. . . ."

But by then, Konrad had already left.

The sun was going down and Konrad was tired. He had never been all alone before—far away from a warm bed and a good meal.

I certainly don't want to go poking in garbage pails or sleeping in doorways; only dogs do that, he thought. Maybe I should go back to the family.

But he really didn't want to go back.

Just then, a little girl and her father walked up to him.

"Hello," said the girl.

"Hello," answered Konrad. "My name's Konrad."

"You're a handsome dog, Konrad."

"I'm not a dog."

"Oh, I beg your pardon."

"What?" asked her surprised father.

"He says he's not a dog."

"Oh, really?" Her father smiled.

"Can I come home with you?" asked Konrad.

"I'll have to ask my father."

"What do you have to ask me?"

"Can Konrad come home with us?" Then she added in a whisper, "I think he's tired and hungry."

"Well, all right...I hope your mother doesn't mind."

But her mother didn't mind. In fact, she was pleased. "I've always wanted a dog," she said.

"Please, Mama, he's not a dog."

"Don't be silly...."

"No, dear," the father said, "Abigail's correct. He's not a dog."

Dinnertime came and the family sat down to eat. Abigail's mother put a bowl of scraps on the floor for Konrad. But Konrad climbed up on a chair at the table and flashed his smile. Her mother looked at Abigail.

"What's this?" she asked.

"Don't insult him. Put the bowl on the table."

So her mother did and Konrad ate very happily.

When bedtime came, Abigail's father offered to put a bit of rug in Abigail's room for the dog. But when he went up there, Konrad was already asleep, snugly tucked under the blankets of Abigail's bed. It was rather crowded.

The next morning, Abigail's mother woke up bright and early and went into the bathroom to brush her teeth. "Eek!" she yelled. Konrad was lying on his back in the tub pretending to take a bath.

Abigail had to go to school and, of course, Konrad insisted
on going along.

"What will your teacher say?" asked her father.

"I'm sure she'll like him too."

So, Konrad accompanied her to school.

"What do you mean by bringing a dog here?" said her teacher.

"He's not a dog."

And her teacher decided that Abigail had a wonderful imagination and allowed Konrad to stay.

A week passed. Konrad had been having a splendid time. Everyone liked him and no one called him a dog—at least in his presence.

But then, something silly happened. All the children told their parents about Konrad. And all their dogs listened. Pretty soon, the dogs started telling the children:

"I'm not a dog."

"Don't call me a dog."

"I want steak, not dog food."

"I'd like a raincoat like yours—and boots."

"What will you get me for my birthday?"

"We're not dogs. We're all going to school with you!"

And the children brought them to school. The classrooms overflowed with dogs. There weren't enough seats or lunches to go around. And the noise was deafening.

"What are all these dogs doing here?" Konrad asked, his nose in the air.

"Listen, buddy, you're one yourself," challenged a boxer.

"I am not."

"Well, whatever you are, do be quiet about *us* being dogs. You'll spoil our fun," a poodle said.

"Dogs don't belong in a classroom," Konrad began, but he was interrupted by the entrance of the principal.

"This is outrageous!" she said. "Something must be done.
All of you take these dogs home at once!"

"They're not dogs!" the children shouted back.

Abigail's teacher told the principal she'd fix things and she
took Abigail aside.

"Look, Abigail," she said, "I know Konrad isn't a dog, but you must take him home. Otherwise, these other dogs won't leave."

"Ms. Marsh, I know he really *is* a dog. It's Konrad who won't believe he is."

"Oh, I see. Then we must convince him."

"But how?"

"Well...."

And they thought of a plan. Then they told the other children about it, and the children told their parents. Everyone hoped it would work.

The next morning, Konrad went down to breakfast, eagerly awaiting his bacon and eggs. Instead, he got a bowl of lumpy oatmeal.

"What's this?" he made a face.

"Oatmeal. People like it—but dogs don't," Abigail said.

"Where's my bacon and eggs?"

"We don't eat that every day."

"Oh," said Konrad. He didn't touch his oatmeal.

"Konrad! You look dirty. You need a bath," Abigail's father said.

"I already had one," answered Konrad.

But Abigail's father didn't hear him. He carried the dog upstairs and plopped him in a bubble bath.

"Ptooey," Konrad spit the soap from his mouth. "Let me out of here." He struggled hard, but he couldn't get away until he was washed and then dried.

"Oatmeal! Ugh!" complained the poodle at school. "I never want to eat *that* for breakfast again."

"Yeah, and I never want to take another bubble bath. They're for sissies," added the boxer.

Konrad didn't say a word.

Ms. Marsh put some math problems on the board. "All right, now class, I want these finished in ten minutes." The dogs, as usual, sat and watched the children work.

"Let me see your papers.... Why, where is yours?" Ms. Marsh said to the poodle. "And yours?" to the boxer. "And *especially* yours, Konrad?"

The dogs began to protest.

"Silence!" cried Ms. Marsh. "You are all punished. No lunch and no play time."

So, while everyone else ate lunch and played outside, the dogs had to sit quietly, their heads on their desks.

By the end of the day, they were all disgusted. "This is for the birds," said the boxer. "I'm going back to being a dog."

"Me too," said the poodle.

"Me too," chorused the others.

While they walked home slowly, Konrad
turned to Abigail.

"Uh...what if I pretended, just pretended
to be a dog?"

"What about it?" said Abigail.

"Would I have to eat oatmeal?"

"No."

"Would I have to take a bubble bath?"

"No."

"Would I have to do arithmetic?"

"No."

Konrad was silent for a while. Then he
said, "Could I chase cats?"

"Yes."

"And bury bones and play Frisbee?"

"Yes, yes."

"And would you still...love me?" he
asked in a very shy voice.

"Oh, Konrad, of course I would."

After a pause, he said, "Okay, then I'll
pretend to be a dog."

The next day, for breakfast, he ate dog food from his own bright plastic dish. He wore a shiny collar and was walked on a long leather leash. Abigail brushed him and patted him and then started for school.

"Bye, Konrad. Be a good dog. I'll see you later."

As he watched her leave, Konrad wanted to run after her, but he didn't.

And when she came home, they went to the park together and ran with the other children and their dogs.

So that's how Konrad, the dog who insisted he wasn't, pretended to be a dog.

And as far as I know, he's still pretending.

MARILYN SINGER wrote this book because "one afternoon, after a hard day at the Brooklyn Museum, I noticed my dog, Konrad, grinning at me. I knew what he was thinking, and put it down on paper. Konrad was delighted. After all, it's his first book too." Ms. Singer, who lives with three dogs, five chinchillas, and thirty-five fancy pigeons, as well as one husband, has been an English teacher and an editor. She has also written scripts for a children's television show.

KELLY OECHSLI has illustrated a number of children's books. In the past he has also done magazine work and decorative design. Born in Butte, Montana, he now lives in a suburb of New York City.

The display type is set in Threadgil Open and the text in Vladimir Alphatype. The art was prepared in pen and ink.